This

Matzah Ball Book

belongs to:

Klutzy   Shmutzy

Kvetchy Shluffy Noshy

noshy Boy

by Anne-Marie Baila Asner

MATZAH BALL BOOKS®

Noshy Boy loves to snack. It's what he does best.

Before meals, during meals and after meals, Noshy Boy always finds a little something extra to nibble on.

Cookies, chips and cake are his favorites, but he'll eat ice cream or candy if they're around.

As you can imagine, after some time of this kind of noshing, Noshy Boy grew bigger.

"I can barely close my pants," cried Noshy Boy.

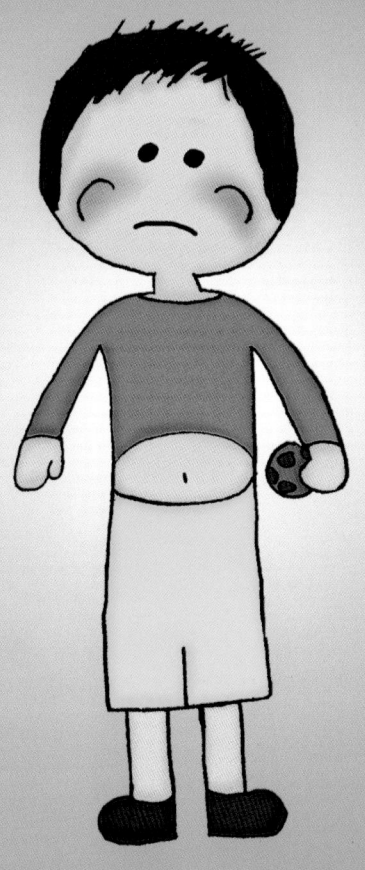

And bigger . . .

"Oh, no! My shirt shrunk!"

He began to panic, "What am I going to do?"

Noshy Boy's big sister, Keppy Girl, is very smart.
She saw her brother was upset and tried to help.

"Noshy Boy, why don't you try going easy on
the sweets?"

"But Keppy Girl, I love to eat. I'm Noshy Boy."

"No one is telling you to stop eating. Just eat better," said Keppy Girl, who reads a lot and usually knows what she's talking about. "Try an apple instead of a cookie, carrots instead of chips, crackers instead of cake."

"But I love cookies, chips and cake," said Noshy Boy.

"You know, Noshy Boy, you might love them more if you ate them less. Cookies, chips and cake are meant to be special treats. They're not special if you eat them all the time."

Noshy Boy grumbled at the thought of missing out on his favorite foods, but he decided to follow his sister's advice.

For the next few weeks, Noshy Boy snacked on fruits, vegetables, crackers and yogurt. Noshy Boy started to shrink and it wasn't because he was getting shorter.

Noshy Boy's shirt covered his stomach again and he could close his pants with ease.

"Wow. My clothes fit," thought Noshy Boy. "And I even have more energy to play."

Noshy Boy ran over to Shluffy Girl's house.

"Wake up, Shluffy Girl. Let's go to the park."

"Isn't it nap time?" asked Shluffy Girl with her eyes closed.

"Come on! Let's go!" insisted Noshy Boy.

But Shluffy Girl was already fast asleep.

As for Noshy Boy's favorite foods, he didn't miss them because he still ate them. He just ate less of them and saved treats for special occasions.

At Kvetchy Boy's birthday party, Noshy Boy was first in line for a piece of cake. One piece, that is, and not two or three.

Now Noshy Boy loves to eat cake and chips and cook-ies AND fruits and vegetables and crackers and yogurt and popcorn and nuts and all kinds of food.

Noshy Boy noshes as much as ever, but he makes healthier choices and feels better for it.

Kvetchy   Shluffy   Noshy

Klutzy   Shmutzy

Glossary

A Bissle (little bit) of Yiddish

Bubbe (bŭ-bē) *n.* grandmother

Keppy (kĕpp-ē) *n.* head; *adj.* smart, using one's head

Kibbitzy (kĭbbĭtz-ē) *v. kibbitz* to joke around; *adj. kibbitzy*

Klutzy (klŭts-ē) *adj.* clumsy

Kvelly (k'vĕll-ē) *v. kvell* to be proud, pleased; *adj. kvelly*

Kvetchy (k'vĕtch-ē) *adj.* whiny, complaining

Noshy (nŏsh-ē) *v. nosh* to snack; *adj. noshy*

Shayna Punim (shā-nă pŭ-nĭm) *adj.* pretty *(shayna); n.* face *(punim)*

Shleppy (shlĕp-ē) *v. shlep* to carry or drag; *adj. shleppy*

Shluffy (shlŭf-ē) *adj.* sleepy, tired

Shmoozy (shmooz-ē) *adj.* chatty, friendly

Shmutzy (shmŭtz-ē) *adj.* dirty, messy

Tushy (tŭsh-ē) *n.* buttocks, bottom

Zaide (zā-dē) *n.* grandfather

For information about Matzah Ball Books, visit
www.matzahballbooks.com

MATZAH BALL BOOKS®

Products

◀ **toddler tee**
sizes: 2T & 4T

youth & adult tees ▶
sizes: S, M, L

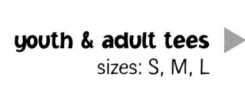

◀ **infant set**

noshy Boy dish set ▶

Shmutzy Girl dish set ▶

HOW TO ORDER:
- website: www.matzahballbooks.com
- e-mail: orders@matzahballbooks.com
- phone: (310) 936-5683